TONY BRADMAN and MARGARET CHAMBERLAIN

LOOK OUT, He's Behind You!

LITTLE
MAMMOTH

This is Little Red Riding Hood, this is her grandmother,

this is the woodcutter, and this is . . .

Little Red Riding Hood is going to see her grandmother.

She goes out of the house and down the road.

She goes round the corner . . .

over the bridge . . .

across the village green . . .

and into the dark, dark wood.

At last, Little Red Riding Hood

goes into Grandmother's cottage.

Is this the end for Little Red Riding Hood?

Who can save her now?

Here are Little Red Riding Hood and her grandmother,

and here is the woodcutter . . .

But where is the big bad wolf?